Chapter 1

Mrs Trouble and the Victorians

Luke had a problem. He wasn't sure if the problem was his new school, his new house, or Mrs Rubble.

School would be OK if it wasn't for Mrs Rubble. Mrs Rubble was Luke's teacher and her favourite subject was History. Luke didn't like History. His favourite subject was Home Time. Oh, and he liked Break Time and Lunch Time too.

"History is stupid," Luke said. "It's all about dead people."

"Yeah," his friend Mohammed said. "Dead people are – well, like, dead."

"Maths is stupid too," Luke went on. "I mean, what's the point? I've got a calculator."

"Yeah." Mohammed nodded. "Maths is ..." Mohammed stopped. What was Maths like?

"It's all numbers," Luke said. "Counting. And writing is stupid too. Why spend hours writing stuff down when you can just *tell* people it all?"

"Yeah, or you could text them," Mohammed said.

"That's like writing it down," Luke pointed out.

Mohammed was silent. He liked writing, and Maths. But he liked Luke more.

"What do you think of Mrs Rubble?" Luke asked.

"Don't know," Mohammed said. "What do you think of her?"

"I think," Luke said, "Mrs Rubble is trouble."

Mohammed laughed. "Yeah. She's Mrs Trouble! What will you do for the History project, Luke?"

Mrs Rubble wanted everyone to do a project about the Victorians. The class had been full of ideas the day she told them about it.

"Mine will be about Jack the Ripper!" Jack shouted. "I'll call it 'Jack the Dripper', because he dripped blood everywhere."

Grace shivered. "Mine will be about Florence Nightingale," she said. "She was a nurse who made people better."

THE GHOST IN THE BATH

JEREMY STRONG

With illustrations by
Scoular Anderson

Barrington Stoke

This is for ghost hunters everywhere. Make sure you always have a bucket of water handy.

First published in 2017 in Great Britain by
Barrington Stoke Ltd
18 Walker Street, Edinburgh, EH3 7LP

www.barringtonstoke.co.uk

This 4u2read edition based on *The Ghost in the Bath*
(Barrington Stoke, 2012)

Text © 2017 Jeremy Strong
Illustrations © 2012 & 2017 Scoular Anderson

A CIP catalogue record for this book is available
from the British Library upon request

ISBN: 978-1-78112-726-1

Printed in China by Leo

Contents

"Jack the Dripper is better," Jack said. "He was a killer who made people worse!"

"You're horrid," said Grace.

"You're stupid," said Jack.

"That's enough," said Mrs Rubble. "I want your projects in by Friday. Luke, what will yours be about?"

Luke's mind went blank. It always went blank when Mrs Rubble spoke to him. He started to shrug but then he had the best idea ever.

"Mine will be about the Vikings!" he said.

"The Vikings lived in Viking times," Mrs Rubble snapped. "The Victorians lived in Victorian times. Find out about them and do your project on them."

Luke sighed. The only thing that happened in History was that everyone died. Sometimes Luke thought it would be OK to be dead. That way he wouldn't have to do stupid projects for Mrs Trouble.

Chapter 2

A Surprise Visitor

When Luke got home he asked his parents what he could do for the History project.

"Jack the Ripper," Dad said.

"Too much blood," Mum said. "What about Florence Nightingale?"

"Floppy Night-Gown!" Dad said. "That's girl stuff."

Luke sighed. His brain felt like a bowl of cold porridge.

"Go and have a bath before bed," Mum said. "Maybe you'll get an idea while you're in there."

"More likely he'll get wet," Dad said, and he laughed at his own joke.

Luke's family's house was about 200 years old and it had an old bathroom too. The tub had four feet like lion paws and very high sides.

Luke put the taps on, took off his clothes and climbed in. He put in some bubble bath to make big, fat bubbles. Then he lay back, closed his eyes and floated away in a dream about a girl. She was tall and pretty and looked at least 18. She asked Luke what he was doing in Charlie's bath.

"I'm not in Charlie's bath," Luke told her. "This is my bath."

The girl stamped her foot. "It's Charlie's bath," she said. "Get out. You're not allowed in Charlie's bath."

"I told you, this isn't Charlie's bath. It's mine," Luke insisted.

The girl reached out to choke Luke with both hands. This wasn't a dream – it was a nightmare! Luke opened his eyes.

"Argh!" Luke yelled.

There WAS a girl in his bath!

Luke hid himself under the bubbles as much as he could. "WHO ARE YOU?" he asked. "How did you get in here? Why are you so ... thin?"

"Who are YOU?" the girl said, hands on hips. "This is my Charlie's house and my Charlie's bath, and you shouldn't be in it. Get out!"

"I can't," Luke said. "You're looking!"

"I won't look," the girl said. "I'll count to ten and then come back." She stepped out of the bath and PING! She vanished.

Luke hopped out, grabbed a HUGE towel and folded it round his body. His mind was turning cartwheels. That girl had vanished, right in front of his eyes. How?

PING! She was back, standing in the bath again.

"You're a ghost!" Luke said.

"Yes," the girl said. "But you can only see me if part of my body is touching water."

"Right," Luke said. "So when you vanished just now, in fact you were still here in the bathroom."

The girl nodded. Luke turned very, VERY red.

"It doesn't matter," the girl said. "I'm a ghost. My name's Ellie, and Charlie and I were going to get married but I drowned."

"You drowned in Charlie's bath?" Luke asked.

"Of course not, stupid," Ellie snapped. "How old are you?"

"Eleven," Luke snapped back.

"Well, you're very silly for an eleven year old," Ellie said.

Luke wondered if Mrs Rubble and Ellie were related in any way.

"Of course I didn't drown in his bath," Ellie said. "I drowned at sea. I was on the *Titanic* when it sank."

Luke's eyes almost popped out of his head. "Wow!" he said. "The *Titanic*? You were on the *Titanic*?"

Ellie nodded, and her face went all sad. "Charlie was on the *Titanic* too. We jumped into the sea together. The water was so cold that we couldn't hold on to each other. Our whole bodies went numb. We slipped away from each other. Everything was dark and cold. I drowned. Charlie must have drowned too."

Luke bit his lip. He didn't know what to say. It was too sad for him to say anything.

"I've been looking for Charlie ever since," Ellie said. "I thought that if I came back to Charlie's house I might find him again. But then you were in his bath. I've got to find Charlie. I won't be at peace until I find him."

Luke swallowed. What a tragic story. He looked at Ellie. She seemed so lost and sad. Then Luke had the best idea ever.

"I'm going to help you find Charlie," he told Ellie. "And, in return, you can help me with my History project. It's about the Victorians. Now I know what to write about – the *Titanic*!"

"But the *Titanic* wasn't Victorian," Ellie said. "Queen Victoria died a few years before it sank."

"A few years won't matter," Luke said. "My teacher won't notice. Victorians, Vikings – they're all the same."

Chapter 3

Fight!

"Have you seen the ghost in the bathroom?" Luke asked Mum at breakfast.

"No," she said. "Is it a nice ghost or a creepy one?" Luke could tell that she didn't believe him.

"She's OK," Luke said. "But I'm never sure when she's there. Dad, how long ago did the *Titanic* sink?"

"1912," Dad said. "Why do you want to know?"

"Just wondered," Luke said. "Mum, could we find out who lived here before us?"

"Maybe you could find out at the library," Mum said. "Is it for your homework?"

Luke grinned. "Yes!"

The library – of course. He'd drop in on his way from school.

When Luke got to class he told Mohammed about the ghost in the bathroom.

"A ghost?" Mohammed said.

Luke nodded.

"And she saw you in the bath?" Mohammed's eyes almost popped out of his head.

Luke nodded again.

"What did you do?" Mohammed asked.

"I said, *Hello, who are you?*" Luke said.

This was not what had happened, but Luke thought it sounded good. "The ghost is going to help me with my History project," he said.

"Wow!" Mohammed said. "I wish I could see a ghost."

"I'll bring her to school," Luke said.

Next thing, Mohammed had told the whole class that Luke was going to bring a ghost into school.

Grace was so shocked she almost tipped a whole tub of fish food into the goldfish bowl. But Jack just sneered.

"I don't believe in ghosts," he said. "It was just your own foot sticking up out of the water." Then he pulled a silly face and ran around going, "Wooooooo!"

"You're stupid," Luke shouted, and they pushed and shoved each other. Luke tripped over his own feet and Jack jumped on top of him.

"Fight! Fight!" the class shouted.

The next minute Mrs Rubble appeared. She pulled Luke and Jack up and demanded to know what the fuss was about. Mohammed told her.

"Whose fault was it?" Mrs Rubble asked.

"His," Luke said, and he pointed at Jack.

"His," Jack said, and he pointed at Luke.

"In that case you can both say 'sorry' to each other," Mrs Rubble said. "Then Luke can stand at one end of the playground and Jack can stand at the other, and there will be no more play for either of you."

Luke stomped off to his end of the playground. 'Jack is an idiot,' he thought. 'I'll get Ellie to come into school. Then he'll be sorry!'

Chapter 4

A Visit to the Library

On his way home from school Luke popped into the library. He'd never seen so many books before. He was sure you could find out about anything in the world here.

There were two women at the main desk. One was young with a tight, thin mouth. When she spoke it looked as if she was trying to snap up flies.

The other woman was about the same age as Mrs Rubble, but with twinkly eyes and a smiley face. She winked at Luke.

"Can I help you?" she asked.

"Children's books are over there," the younger one snapped.

"I don't want a children's book," Luke whispered. "I want to know who lived in my house in the past."

"We're not detectives," the younger woman snapped, but the older lady waved at Luke to follow her into the building.

"My name is Betty," she told Luke as they walked. "We keep records about people from this area on the computer. What's the name of the road you live in?"

Betty typed in the name of Luke's road and his house number. "Oh," she said as she read the screen. "Your house is quite old, isn't it?"

"Dad says it's 200 years old," Luke said.

"That means a lot of people have lived there," Betty said. "Was there any special date you had in mind?"

Luke shut his eyes. When did the *Titanic* sink? Think, brain, think!

"1912!" he shouted with a grin.

Betty scanned the screen. "Here we are," she said. "Edward and Flora Smith lived there then. It says here that they had five children. Daisy, Elsie, Peter, Charles and Susan."

"Charles! Charlie!" Luke said. "His name was Charlie Smith."

"There." Betty smiled. "You've found him."

"I want to know what happened to him," Luke said.

"Right," Betty said. "We need to look at another set of records. Hang on a minute ... These are the records of births and deaths."

Luke typed in CHARLES SMITH. Oh dear – there were records for 23 Charles Smiths.

"Never mind," Betty said. "The records will show his address. Can you see it?"

"There!" Luke said, and he jabbed a finger at the screen. "Charles Smith. Wounded in France, died 15th March, 1915." He looked again. "1915," he said, in a soft voice.

"That was the middle of the First World War," Betty said. "He was wounded in France, in the war, and he died when he got home."

"So he didn't drown," Luke said.

"Oh no," Betty said. "I expect he got shot, or blown up, or gassed. It was a terrible war. Is it important?"

Luke shook his head. "I don't know," he said. "Only Ellie can answer that question."

"Who's Ellie?" Betty asked, and she winked again. "Is she your girlfriend?"

Luke almost choked. "No," he said. "She's just – she's just someone who hangs around where she's not wanted."

"Oh," said Betty.

"And she's wet," Luke added.

Chapter 5

More of Ellie

When Luke got home he went to the bathroom and locked himself in.

"Ellie?" he called. "Are you there?"

At last a faint shape began to appear. It was Ellie, or at least some of Ellie. All Luke could see was one half of her body, and half her head. And she was standing in the toilet bowl.

"Yuck!" Luke said. "Do you have to stand there?"

"Yes. I have to be in contact with water, remember?" Ellie said.

"But I can only see half of you," Luke moaned.

"I need lots of water to make a full appearance," Ellie told him. "That's why I stood in the bath before."

"You're weird," Luke said. "Ghosts don't appear in toilet bowls."

"Oh, you're an expert on ghosts now, are you?" Ellie asked. Then her lip wobbled. "Do you think I want to be like this?" she said. "I didn't want to drown and I never wanted to be a ghost. It's not much fun."

Luke was shocked. He thought it would be ace to be a ghost. You could scare people. Cool! But then he remembered he had something to tell Ellie. "I've discovered more about Charlie," he said. "He didn't drown."

Ellie's hand flew to her mouth. "Do you know what happened to him?" she asked.

"Two years after you drowned there was a war," Luke said. "Charlie went to France to fight, and he was killed."

"Oh," Ellie said softly. "Poor Charlie."

"It was three years after the *Titanic* sank," Luke told her. "I also checked – Charlie wasn't married when he died."

Ellie gave a small smile and then asked Luke if he knew where Charlie was buried. Luke shook his head.

"Betty at the library said I would need to check the church records to find that out. I'll do that tomorrow. I have to do my homework now. I told someone at school about you. They don't believe you're a ghost."

"I bet it was a boy," Ellie said in a smug voice.

"You're right," Luke said. "It was Jack. How did you know?"

"Boys are like that," Ellie said. "Stupid. But not you. Thank you for finding out all those things for me."

Luke was silent for a moment. "I told the boys that you'd come into school with me tomorrow," he said at last. "They'll have to believe in you then. I'll take a big bucket of water and you can stand in it. I can't wait to see Jack's face!"

"No," Ellie said. "I'm not going to your silly school."

"But you've got to!" Luke said.

"No I haven't," Ellie told him. "I'm not a zoo animal you can put on show."

"Well, don't expect me to find Charlie then!" Luke shouted. He was so angry. He stared at

Ellie, standing in the toilet, and his eyes blazed.
Huh! He'd teach her a lesson.

He reached forward and pulled the chain.
Then he stormed out as the toilet flushed.

Chapter 6

More Trouble from Mrs Rubble

The next day, Mrs Rubble asked how their projects were coming on.

"I've finished," Mohammed said, and he beamed at everyone.

"Grace?" Mrs Rubble asked.

"I've done six pages," Grace said. "And I've found some photos of Florence Nightingale."

"How thrilling," Jack said under his breath, only everyone heard him.

Mrs Rubble fixed Jack with her steely eyes.

"I've done three pictures of Jack the Ripper murdering people and blood spurting out of their necks," Jack said.

Mrs Rubble's eyebrows shot up her head. "I see. Perhaps you could do some writing too, without the blood. Now, Luke, what about you?"

"I'm collecting information," Luke said. He hoped that would be enough for Mrs Rubble. It wasn't.

"And what have you found out?" she asked.

"Um ..." Luke began. "I know who used to live in my house 100 years ago."

"That sounds interesting. Do you know their name?"

"Charlie Smith," Luke said. "He was going to marry a girl called Ellie."

"Yeah, but Ellie drowned and now she's a ghost," Mohammed said. The rest of the class laughed.

"Yeah, and Luke said he'd bring the ghost to school," Jack shouted. "Only she's not here, because there's no such thing as ghosts. Luke's just a baby who believes in ghosts!"

"I am not!" Luke shouted, and his face went all red.

"Wooooo!" Jack mocked.

"That's enough!" Mrs Rubble shouted. "It's Friday tomorrow and your projects have to be in. I expect your work on my desk first thing in the morning."

Luke was in a bad mood all day. It wasn't fair. It was all Ellie's fault. She was such a pain.

But as the day went on, Luke thought about Ellie more and more. What was it like to drown? Horrible. Scary too. And she lost Charlie, and he lost her. Poor Charlie. He survived the *Titanic* only to be killed in a war. Now Ellie was stuck in Charlie's old house trying to find him so she could be at peace. And only Luke could help her.

After school Luke took the long way home past three different churches. The first church was locked up. The second church was open and Luke went in. It was dark and cold and smelled a bit. A woman came out of the gloom.

"I'm the vicar," she told Luke. "Can I help?"

Luke told her he needed to find out who was buried in the area.

"I'm afraid I can't tell you," the vicar said.
"Only adults can look at the records."

Luke nodded. "I'll just have to wait ten years then," he said. The vicar gave him a blank look. "That was a joke," Luke told her.

The same thing happened at the third church.

Luke was fed up with everything. He hadn't done his project. He had nothing to show Mrs Rubble. He had no idea where Charlie was buried. He was useless.

At home he ran a bath for Ellie and soon she appeared. He could see all of her this time.

"What did you find out?" she asked, with a keen look on her face.

"Nothing." Luke told her about the church visits.

"You tried," Ellie said. "Thank you."

"Yeah, and now everybody thinks I'm stupid and a liar because you didn't come to school with me today," Luke said. "Jack says ghosts don't exist. And I haven't done my project."

Ellie frowned. "What if we give them all a shock?" she asked. "What if I come to school with you tomorrow?"

"Really?" Luke asked. He felt better at once.

Ellie smiled. "I don't really want to, but you've tried to help me and it would be fun to do something silly," she said.

Luke was ready to burst. "It'll be ace!" he said. "I'll find the biggest bucket ever and you can stand in that. It will be so cool!"

Chapter 7

Buckets Galore!

At breakfast the next day Luke told his parents that everyone in his class had to take a bucket into school.

"All of you?" Mum asked. "Mrs Rubble wants 27 buckets?"

"Yes," Luke lied. He had his fingers crossed under the table so the lie didn't count.

Mum looked at Dad. Dad looked at Mum. They both looked at Luke.

"We don't have any buckets," Mum said.
"I've got this yoghurt pot. I could clean that out
for you."

Luke's heart sank. What good would that
be? He could just imagine Ellie trying to stand
in a yoghurt pot. He stomped off to school in
a very, very bad mood, with an invisible Ellie
beside him. Luke knew she was there because
she was making such a fuss.

"You're useless," Ellie moaned. "I wish I
hadn't bothered. I wish I'd never seen you in

the bath. I wish I'd never said I'd go to your school. I wish ..."

"I wish you'd shut up!" Luke shouted, as they passed the bus stop. Six people turned to stare at him.

"Who are you telling to shut up?" an old man demanded.

Luke hurried on. "Shh!" he hissed to Ellie. "You're getting me into trouble."

"Huh! All you do is think about yourself," Ellie snapped. "I *drowned*!"

They sank into a black silence after that. Luke wondered what he would do when they reached school. If he couldn't get enough water no one would see Ellie and everyone would laugh at him.

As Luke walked into class, Jack grinned and went "Woooooooo!" and a few children giggled. Mrs Rubble glared at them over her glasses.

"Time to see what you've done for your projects," she said. "Please hold up your work so I can see it."

And 26 hands went up with 26 projects. Mrs Rubble's eyes scanned the room.

"Luke," she said. "You don't seem to have any work in your hand. Have you done it?"

"Yes," said Luke.

"It must be invisible then," Mrs Rubble said.

Luke almost laughed. That was the problem. His project – Ellie – *was* invisible!

"Luke, can you please explain why you have nothing to show?" Mrs Rubble said.

Luke took a deep breath. There was nothing for it but to tell the truth. So he stood up and told Mrs Rubble and everyone about the bathroom and Ellie and the *Titanic*.

Jack began to snigger. Grace began to laugh. Soon the whole class was chuckling away as if the whole thing was the best joke ever. Of course, it would have helped if Ellie had spoken up for Luke, but she was still in a huff.

Luke got crosser and crosser and hotter and hotter and redder and redder. He couldn't bear all that laughter banging away in his ears.

"A ghost that can only appear when she's wet?" Mrs Rubble said. "Luke, I have heard lots of mad excuses for not doing homework, but that is the maddest ever!"

"It's true!" Luke shouted, but the class just laughed even louder. "All I need is a bucket of water!"

"A bucket of water!" Mrs Rubble said. She had to sit down she was laughing so hard. Tears ran down her cheeks.

That was it. Luke had had enough. He stormed to the front of the class, grabbed the goldfish bowl and threw it at Ellie. It was a shame Mrs Rubble was sitting behind Ellie because she got soaked too. But it worked. All of a sudden, there was Ellie, standing in a pool of water with a fat goldfish in her hand.

"Oh my!" Mrs Rubble cried, and she fainted.

"Oh!" Grace moaned, and she fainted too.

Jack was silent. That was because he'd fainted ages before.

Chapter 8

Charlie's Grave

Ellie stood there, soaked to the skin, and completely visible. Luke looked at the class with their open mouths and goggle eyes. He smiled, put some water in the bowl and held it out so Ellie could drop the goldfish in.

"This is Ellie," he said. "She drowned when the *Titanic* sank. Now she needs to find where Charlie Smith is buried because they were about to get married. Ellie can't rest in peace until she finds Charlie again."

The class stared in silence.

51

"It's all right," Luke said. "You can talk to her."

"Yes, say something!" Ellie said. "Stop looking at me like I'm a ... ghost." She giggled.

"Are ... you ... really ... dead?" asked Jack, who had woken from his faint.

"Are ... you ... really ... stupid?" Ellie answered back. "Of course I'm dead. Look at me!"

Jack said nothing. Mrs Rubble had come round, so Luke explained about his project.

"I've been doing my project with Ellie," he said. "She's going to tell you what it was like on the *Titanic* when it sank."

And that is what Ellie did, and she did it very well. She brought every moment of the sinking to life. When she got to the bit when she and Charlie lost their grip on each other

and she drowned, almost everyone was in tears.
Mrs Rubble did a lot of sniffing.

At the end the children clapped.

Then Jack said, "Hey, why don't we split up after school and go to all the graveyards to search for Charlie Smith's grave?"

Luke was pleased and cross at the same time. It was a great idea, but he wished he'd thought of it himself.

"Jack's not as stupid as I thought," Ellie said, which made Luke even crosser.

After school the children went on a grave hunt and soon Grace came back with some good news. She had found a grave with Charlie Smith's name on it, and the right date – 1915. Ellie had dried off by this time. Luke had to hunt round the graveyard until he found a watering can beside a tap. He used it to give her a good sprinkling and they could see her again.

"At last," Ellie sighed. "Charlie and I can be together at last." She turned to Luke and the class. "Thank you," she said. "Thank you for everything."

Ellie hovered over the old grave for a minute and then very slowly, bit by bit, she sank into the ground. Her feet vanished first, then her legs, her body and her smiling face. At last she was gone. There was nothing but the peace and quiet of the old graveyard.

When Luke had a bath that night he covered himself in plenty of bubbles, just in case. But there was no sign of Ellie. But he did get a surprise when he went into school on Monday morning.

Mrs Rubble was sitting at her desk with a rather evil smile on her face.

"Luke," she began. "I think we have a problem. You didn't do your project last week."

"Yes I did!" Luke said. "It was Ellie and the *Titanic*!"

"Exactly!" Mrs Rubble cried. "The *Titanic* sank in 1912. That was 11 years after Queen

Victoria died, so it did NOT happen in Victorian times!"

Luke was gobsmacked. He'd brought a real ghost to school and it still wasn't enough for Mrs Rubble!

Mohammed put up his hand. "Mrs Rubble, Luke did do his project. Ellie was 18 when she died, which means she was born 7 years BEFORE Queen Victoria died. Ellie was a Victorian."

"Yes!" the class cried. "Ellie was a Victorian. So there!"

"OK," Mrs Rubble muttered. "Don't get your knickers in a twist. Luke's done his project."

Luke sighed in relief. He wasn't very good at History. He wasn't much better at Maths. It was a good thing Mohammed was there to help him.

Luke winked at Mohammed and his friend beamed back a broad smile.